Moonfleet

A classic tale of smuggling

Based on the novel by
J.M. Falkner

Adapted by Rob Lloyd Jones

Illustrated by Alan Marks

Reading Consultant: Alison Kelly
Roehampton University

In the middle of the 18th century, smugglers lurked around the south coast of England. These were men who hid goods brought from other countries, so they didn't have to pay taxes on them. Government officials, known as magistrates, did everything they could to stop the smugglers – even if that meant killing them.

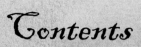

Contents

Chapter 1
Moonfleet village

My name is John Trenchard, and I was fifteen years old when this story began, on a stormy night in Moonfleet village. Fierce winds swept from the sea, shaking our houses, shattering windows, and sending tiles flying from roofs. In the bay, huge waves broke over the cliffs, flooding the cobbled streets.

The next morning, we had to tiptoe through mud as the church bells called us to the Sunday service. We all sat wrapped up in thick coats as Mr. Glennie, the minister, began his sermon. Suddenly, a strange noise echoed around the walls – a knocking sound, like boats jostling at sea. Everyone jumped up, listening to the eerie noises. They were coming from the vault under the church.

"It's Blackbeard!" someone shouted.

Everyone shuddered. Blackbeard was the nickname of John Mohune, a rich noble who owned the village over a hundred years ago. His tomb sat beneath the church, but many villagers believed his ghost still haunted Moonfleet, protecting treasure he had buried before he died.

Mr. Glennie just laughed. "The noises aren't ghosts," he said. "The floods have filled the vault with water, and the sounds are coffins banging against each other as they float."

Still, I wasn't convinced. The coffins in the vault were a hundred years old, and would surely be rotten by now. The noises we'd heard sounded like solid wood.

The entrance to Blackbeard's vault was around the back of the church, so after the service I crept outside to investigate. The floodwaters had turned the ground into a muddy slush, and the gravestones were tangled with foul-smelling seaweed. I scraped some off the door to the vault. Usually, the heavy stone entrance was sealed shut, but the floods had forced it open. To my amazement, I could see a dark tunnel leading under the church.

All I could think about was Blackbeard's treasure. Could it be hidden inside his vault? I was desperate to find out. But I would have to go home for a candle and, anyway, I was late for lunch. I decided to return later to hunt for the treasure.

Chapter 2
The secret vault

Back home, Aunt Jane greeted me with a scowl. "You're late John," she snapped. "Your lunch is cold now."

My parents had died when I was very young, and I had lived with my aunt ever since. She was a stern woman, who rarely allowed me out of the house. So, that night, I waited until I heard her snoring in her room, then grabbed a candle and slipped out in secret.

I was so excited about the treasure, I didn't even feel scared until I reached the churchyard. Then I remembered the noises from beneath the church, and the stories of Blackbeard's ghost. But the lure of treasure drew me on, and soon I was back at the entrance to Blackbeard's vault.

I lit the candle and stepped inside. My heart was pounding as I followed a tunnel to a set of steps that curved under the church. At the bottom lay a dark chamber.

Inside, several old coffins lay on shelves around the walls. But the floor of the vault was filled with brand new barrels. To my horror, I realized I had discovered a smugglers' hideout. It must have been these barrels that had made the noises we heard in church.

I had to get out – smugglers were dangerous men, who didn't look kindly on spying eyes. But, as I turned to go, I heard a voice in the tunnel. Someone was coming!

I quickly snuffed out my candle, and hid
behind a coffin as two men entered the vault
and set down some more barrels. Peeking over
the edge, I saw that one of them was the
church groundskeeper, Ratsey, and the other
was Elzivir Block, who owned a local inn called
the *Why Not*. Last year, his son David had
been shot and killed by Maskew, a local
magistrate who had caught him smuggling.

Eventually, the smugglers left and I climbed from my hiding place. Dizzy from the stale vault air, I slipped and knocked the lid from a coffin. Inside, a body lay wrapped in cloth. Part of it was torn, and I could see bushy black hair around the figure's neck. I was sure it was Blackbeard. Could his treasure be inside the coffin?

With trembling hands, I relit the candle. A silver locket hung around Blackbeard's neck. I lifted it away, hoping to find some jewels inside, but all it held was a scrap of paper with what seemed to be a prayer written on it.

Disappointed, I looped the locket around my neck and returned along the tunnel. But now I discovered the entrance had been sealed. The smugglers must have covered it when they left. I pushed at the stone blocking my way out, but I couldn't shift it.

Now I realized why I had felt dizzy – there was no air here underground. Crazy with panic, I bashed at the door, screaming for help. But it was no good. My candle burned out. Everything went dark and I fell to the floor.

Chapter 3
Elzivir Block

I woke to find myself lying in bed. At first I thought that everything had been a dream, but then I felt the locket around my neck and knew I had been rescued.

The door creaked open, and Elzivir Block came in. I thought he would be furious that I had found his smugglers' den, but instead he smiled and handed me a bowl of soup. As I drank it, he told me how he and Ratsey had heard my shouts from the vault. They had raced back and found me lying unconscious inside. I was now upstairs in Elzivir's inn, the *Why Not*.

"You can stay here until you're well again," Elzivir said.

I stayed in bed for several days. All the time, Elzivir looked after me like a nurse. I had always thought he was stern and fierce, but I have never known anyone kinder than he was then.

Elzivir had already told my aunt where I was, but when I finally returned to her house, she refused to let me in. "You chose to run away," she snapped, "so now you can *stay* away."

I was homeless. The only friend I had was Elzivir, so I returned to the *Why Not* and told him what had happened.

"You must live here then," he said. "There's plenty of room."

So, I began to live with Elzivir at the old tavern. In the mornings I went to school, but I spent my afternoons helping him in the gardens or with his boats in the bay. Elzivir had lived alone since his son died, and I think he was glad for the company. He rarely mentioned David, but spoke often about his hatred for Mr. Maskew, the magistrate who killed him.

One afternoon, I was walking in the woods when I met Maskew's daughter, Grace. I knew Grace Maskew from school. She was pretty and kind and I had always liked her. As we walked together, I couldn't help telling her everything that had happened. Grace looked worried.

"John," she said, "please be careful."

I knew what Grace meant. Elzivir was a smuggler, and now that I was living with him, she thought I might become one myself. Grace's father hated smugglers, and was determined to rid Moonfleet of them all. One evening, I discovered just how determined he was.

Elzivir and I were playing cards in the *Why Not*, when the magistrate burst through the door, his long coat flapping in the breeze.

Elzivir leapt up, his face red with rage. "You're not welcome in my house," he cried.

"Your house?" Maskew said, "Not for long!" and he threw a piece of paper onto the bar.

Elzivir read it in silence, then handed it to me. It was about the *Why Not*. He had never owned the tavern, but rented it from a local landlord. Now Maskew had offered the landlord more money than Elzivir to buy it for himself.

"I want you both out by next week," he said, slamming the door as he left.

Elzivir threw Maskew's letter on the fire and sparks crackled up the chimney.

"Elzivir," I cried, "what will we do? We don't have enough money to keep the *Why Not*."

"There is one way," Elzivir replied. "A smugglers' ship is bringing a new cargo into Hoar Head Bay tomorrow night. It's a heavy load, and the job will pay well for the men who help carry it ashore. Will you join us?"

Smuggling! The thought terrified me, but Elzivir had been so kind, I was determined not to let him down. "I will," I said, trying to sound confident.

That night, I met Grace in the woods, and told her the news. She was still worried about the danger of smuggling, and scared I might get caught.

"It's only once," I promised her, "and when I return, I'll have made my own money."

"Then I'll keep a candle burning in my window until you do," she said.

Chapter 4
Hoar Head Bay

It was midnight when Elzivir and I reached Hoar Head Bay. Several other smugglers were already on the beach, hiding in the shadows by the cliff. Seeing that I was with Elzivir, they greeted me as a friend.

"The ship should arrive soon," they told me. "Wait with us."

Several hours passed. I sat beside some rocks, fidgeting with nerves. At last, there came a shout. "The ship," someone yelled. "It's here!"

Everyone rushed to pull the ship up onto the pebbly beach. Heavy barrels, filled with brandy, were passed down from the deck and packed into carts. Soon they were all unloaded, and the ship was heading back out to sea. Just then, one of the smugglers spotted a figure hiding among some rocks. "Over there," he cried. "A spy!"

Several of the smugglers chased off after the figure. A few minutes later, they returned dragging a prisoner – Mr. Maskew!
"Shoot him," someone said.

"Don't touch him," Elzivir shouted. "Leave him with me, and go your ways."

Everyone knew that Maskew had killed Elzivir's son. Now was his chance for revenge. Taking the barrels, the smugglers left us alone with our prisoner.

Elzivir raised a pistol to the magistrate's head. His hand shook with rage.

"Spare me, Mr. Block," Maskew grovelled. "Oh, spare me please!"

"Elzivir," I pleaded. "Don't shoot!" I hated Maskew too, but I couldn't let Elzivir kill him – he was Grace's father.

Elzivir looked at me, and I saw his pistol lower. Then a shout came from above.

"Stop! In the name of the King!" Dozens of soldiers appeared at the top of the cliff.

"Over here," Maskew yelled. "Save me!"

The soldiers raised their rifles and fired. Elzivir and I dived away, but the bullets tore into Mr. Maskew, killing him instantly.

"Run for the cliffs," Elzivir shouted.

I began to run, but the soldiers fired again and a bullet hit my leg. Elzivir rushed over and lifted me up. The pain was incredible.

"I'm sorry, John," he said, "but the soldiers will think we killed Maskew. If they catch us, we will hang for sure."

The only escape was a narrow
path that zig-zagged up the steep side
of a cliff. Below us was a huge drop, but
Elzivir never slipped and never let me fall.
When we reached the top, I lay on the soft
grass, gasping with pain.

"We must keep moving, lad," Elzivir said.
"Those soldiers will find a way up soon enough."

Elzivir lifted me onto his back and we
continued, crossing fields and streams, until we
reached an old stone quarry and the entrance
to a cave.

Inside, water trickled through cracks in the rocky roof. Elzivir gave me some to drink and made a fire. "We can hide here until your leg is healed," he said. "Then we must find passage overseas on a smuggling ship."

Several weeks passed as my leg recovered. Elzivir cleaned the wound each day and talked to me to keep my mind off the pain. He had to risk leaving the cave to find us food, and was sometimes gone for several days at a time.

Alone at night, the cave terrified me. The wind screamed through the entrance, and the fire cast eerie shadows around the walls. I sat clutching the locket I had stolen from Blackbeard's coffin, and read the prayer written inside. I hoped it would guard me against evil spirits.

Then, one night, I noticed something strange about the writing. Four of the words were written in darker ink than the others.

From eight to eighty I shall trek
Until my feet are tired and worn
But as I walk down life's hard road
God's love will keep me well and warm

As I stared at the words, my thoughts returned to Blackbeard's treasure. Was this a code to reveal its hiding place? When I showed Elzivir, his eyes lit up.

"John," he said, "before Blackbeard came to Moonfleet, he lived in Carisbrook Castle. The castle is a prison now, but I have heard that there is a deep well inside!"

"Elzivir," I cried, "the treasure must be hidden in that well – eighty feet down."

Chapter 5
The well

Dark clouds rumbled over Carisbrook Castle as we approached. Elzivir rang a bell beside the huge iron gate. Moments later, it creaked open and the prison guard grinned at us with dirty brown teeth. We had met him in secret the night before, and he'd agreed to take us to the prison's well in exchange for a share of the treasure. He had a shifty look about him that I didn't trust, but we had no choice. "Come on," he snarled. "Hurry up!"

29

We followed him along a dark corridor, and
I heard prisoners moaning inside their cells.
The guard unlocked one of the old doors and
heaved it open. Inside, a barred window let in
enough light to see a dark hole in the floor,
with a dirty bucket hanging above it on a rope.
I peered into the grimy pit, remembering
Blackbeard's message – eighty feet down.
Below, the murky darkness seemed to go
on forever.

"There's the well," the guard said. "Now, where's this treasure?"

"We think it's in this well," I said. "I'm the lightest, so why don't you both lower me down in the bucket? If you stop when you've let out eighty feet of rope, I should be in the right place."

"John," Elzivir whispered, "be careful. I have already lost my son. I would rather lose all the treasure in the world than lose you too."

I climbed into the bucket, and Elzivir and the guard lowered me into the dreadful depths. Above, the hole grew smaller and smaller.

"John," Elzivir shouted finally, "you're eighty feet deep now."

Raising the guard's lamp, I looked around. The bricks were mossy and worn with age. But, as I leaned closer to the wall, I noticed that one of them was not as old as the others. My heart raced – had I found it? I carefully pulled the brick from the wall. Behind it was a small gap... and in it sat a tiny bag. My fingers trembled as I pulled it out and peered inside.

"Have you found anything?" the guard shouted.

Inside the bag was a huge diamond, the size of a walnut.

"Yes," I shouted, "I've found the treasure! Pull me up!"

As soon as I reached the top, I jumped from the bucket, holding up the bag triumphantly. Then I froze – the guard was pointing a pistol right at me. "Give me the treasure," he growled, "or I'll kill you."

Suddenly, Elzivir leapt at him and they fell
into a savage fight. The guard was bigger than
Elzivir, but not as strong. Just as he charged
again, Elzivir flipped him over his shoulder. I
heard a terrible scream as the guard plunged
into the well and fell to his death.

"Quickly John," Elzivir cried, "another guard
might come."

The prison gates slammed shut behind us as
we raced away with the treasure.

Chapter 6
The diamond dealer

That night, Elzivir arranged for a ship to take us to The Hague, a city in Holland. He had heard that it was a good place to sell jewels. I sat on deck, holding the diamond and watching it sparkle in the moonlight. Elzivir stared at the stone too, but he looked worried.

"John," he said, "ever since you first looked for that treasure, luck has run against you. I think that diamond is cursed."

But I didn't listen. Instead, I thought about how I would return to Moonfleet a rich man and marry Grace.

In The Hague, we learned that the richest diamond dealer, a man named Mr. Aldobrand, lived in a huge white mansion on the outskirts of the town. I knocked on the door, and an old man with wrinkled skin answered.

"Are you Mr. Aldobrand?" I asked. "We've come all the way from Moonfleet with a diamond to sell."

The old man plucked the jewel from my hand, and studied it for a long moment.

"Come in then," he said finally.

Mr. Aldobrand led us along a hallway, where several guards sat watching us suspiciously.

"Don't worry about them," Mr. Aldobrand muttered, "they're just for security."

He guided us into a study filled with dusty books. The sun was just setting and its red light fell through the large bay windows. Mr. Aldobrand sat at a desk inspecting the diamond with a magnifying glass as I fidgeted with suspense.

"Well," I asked, "how much is it worth?"

"Nothing," Mr. Aldobrand said. "I am sorry, but this diamond is a fake. It's glass."

"Fake?" I said. "That's not possible!"

"I assure you it is," he replied. "But I will still pay you ten pounds for it."

Elzivir snatched the jewel from the desk. "We did not come here for pennies," he cried. "I am glad to be rid of the thing!" And he hurled the diamond out of the window.

I watched in horror as the jewel landed in a flowerbed outside. Elzivir stormed off, but as I went to follow him, I caught Mr. Aldobrand looking to see where the diamond landed too.

Outside, I told Elzivir what I had seen.

"I don't think the diamond is fake at all," I said. "Mr. Aldobrand was lying to buy it cheaply. We have to find it before he does."

Elzivir gripped my shoulders and looked me in the eye. I had never seen him so serious. "John," he said, "that diamond is cursed. Let it be."

How desperately I wish that I had listened to him, but instead I crept off down the side of the house, and climbed a wall into Mr. Aldobrand's garden. Elzivir followed in silence.

It was darker now, though there was still enough moonlight to look for the diamond. But when I reached the flowerbed where it had landed, the jewel was gone.

"Elzivir," I whispered. "Mr. Aldobrand has already taken it."

"Then let us go home," Elzivir pleaded.

"No," I said. "He must have it inside the house."

Before Elzivir could stop me, I ran to the back of the house and peeked through a gap in the curtains. Inside, Mr. Aldobrand sat at his desk. He had a self-satisfied grin on his face... and our diamond in his hand.

Rage built up inside me. I hurled myself forward, smashing through the window and into the study.

"Thieves!" Mr. Aldobrand screeched. "Help!"

I grabbed the diamond from him, but the door crashed open and Aldobrand's guards charged in carrying clubs. Three of them attacked Elzivir, and two came for me, raining blows on us with sticks and fists. The last thing I saw was the diamond falling to the floor, and then I did the same.

Chapter 7
Prisoners

Elzivir and I were thrown into a cold prison cell and left in the dark. I slumped in a corner, aching from the blows from the guards' clubs.

Several days later, the door burst open and guards marched us to a courthouse. There, Mr. Aldobrand told the judge that we had broken into his house to steal his diamond.

"Liar!" I shouted, but a guard struck me on the head.

"You are both greedy thieves," the judge said, "and I sentence you to work on a chain gang – for the rest of your lives."

As the guards led us away, I leaned over to Mr. Aldobrand. "Now you have the treasure," I told him, "and may it curse you the way it has me."

Elzivir and I were shackled in irons and
marched with hundreds of other criminals to
a place called Ymeguen, where we were made
to build a new fortress. Guards stood by with
whips and guns as we toiled in the blistering
summer sun.

Elzivir was put to work on a different part
of the building, so I barely saw him any more.
Instead, I worked alone, thinking about the
pain I had caused him, and how much I
missed Grace back in Moonfleet.

Ten years later, when I was 26, the fortress was finally finished. One morning, the guards handed some of us over to soldiers, who led us onto a ship at a nearby dock. "Please, where are we going?" I begged one of them.

"Java," he laughed, and lashed me with his whip.

My heart broke. Java was a slave colony on the other side of the world. No prisoner who went there ever returned.

The guards shoved us onto the ship and into a tiny room below deck. Another group of prisoners was already down there, crammed in like pigs in a pen. As my eyes adjusted to the dark, I thought I saw a familiar face. It was Elzivir! His hair was turning white, and his body looked old and tired, but he still found a smile for me.

"I am sorry Elzivir," I cried, hugging him. "I am so sorry."

After that, there was little to say. We were sailing to become slaves on the other side of the world. All hope was gone of ever seeing Grace, Moonfleet or freedom again.

The journey was terrible. There was little light or air below deck and, as the sea grew rougher, many of the prisoners became badly seasick. A week passed, and the weather grew worse. The ship rolled violently over the waves, tossing us about. Then, one night, the hatch above us opened and a guard peered down. His face was white with fear.

"Abandon ship," he cried. "We're sinking!"

Chapter 8
Shipwreck

Elzivir and I scrambled up to the deck. All around us, waves rose up like mountains. The guards had gone – and taken all the lifeboats with them.

"They've left us to die like rats," Elzivir spat. But now I saw something else. There, in the distance, was a line of cliffs.

"Elzivir," I shouted, "those cliffs… We're in Moonfleet Bay!"

Elzivir spotted the cliffs too and a brief smile
flashed across his face. Battling against the
crashing waves, he climbed up to the ship's
steering wheel. "We're not safe yet," he cried,
"I'll try to turn us inland."

There were rocks everywhere and the storm
was getting worse. The other prisoners were
wild with fear. But, gradually, the ship began
to turn.

"John," Elzivir shouted, "look!" He pointed to a small light, flickering on the cliff top. My heart soared. Grace said she would burn a candle until I returned. Had she waited all this time?

We drew closer and closer to the shore. But then I heard a deafening crash.

"We've hit the rocks," Elzivir shouted. The ship flipped on its side, throwing us all headlong into the sea. Waves hammered down on us. I could see villagers calling from the beach, desperate to help. We had little chance of swimming that far, but we had to try.

"It's now or never, John," Elzivir yelled. "God save us both!"

We swam for our lives. I saw the villagers throwing a rope for us to catch, then Elzivir grabbing it. He reached out for me, but I heard a thunder from behind and another great wave smashed me to the shallow seabed.

I thought I was going to die, but then someone dragged me back to the surface. It was Elzivir. He had let go of the rope and swum back to save me.

Elzivir pulled me through the waves, swimming for the shore. "The rope," he shouted, "grab the rope, John!"

The villagers' rope was only an arm's length away. Just as another wave came, Elzivir shoved me forward with all his might. There was a roar of water and I caught the rope. I felt the line pull, and in seconds I was lying safe on the beach.

I looked for Elzivir, but the wave had dragged him back out to sea. I tried to call his name, but I was numb with cold.

Tears poured down my cheeks as I stared out at the crashing waves. Elzivir had drowned. He had given up his life, here on Moonfleet beach, for me.

Chapter 9
The letter

Morning was breaking as I walked up through Moonfleet village. The storm had died and clouds had given way to a brilliant blue sky. The village looked the same as it had years ago. There was my aunt's house, the church, and the *Why Not* inn. I entered the old tavern, and found it cobwebbed and empty. I lit a fire, then sat with my head in my hands, crying for Elzivir.

After a while, I felt a light touch on my shoulder. "John," a voice said, "I kept a candle burning for you. But have you forgotten me?"

It was Grace, grown up and more beautiful than ever. She sat with me, and I told her everything that had happened since I last left Moonfleet. "Grace," I said, "I am a broken wretch, with no money."

Grace just smiled and took my hand. "John," she replied, "it is not money that makes a man. Elzivir was right. That treasure was cursed. And if you ever find it again, you must use it to help others."

I was about to ask her what she meant, when Ratsey came in with Mr. Glennie, the minister. Both had grown old, but I recognized them immediately. I told Ratsey how Elzivir had died, and saw tears in his eyes. Then Mr. Glennie unfolded an old letter.

"John, do you know someone named Mr. Aldobrand?" he asked.

"Only too well," I replied, startled. I told them about the old diamond dealer, and how he had lied to send Elzivir and me to slavery.

"Well," Mr. Glennie said, "this letter is from him. It arrived here eight years ago. After you last saw him, his business collapsed. His health failed too, and he told people you had put a curse on him in court."

I remembered my words in the courthouse. *Now you have the treasure, and may it curse you the way it has me.*

"But what have his fortunes to do with me?" I asked.

"Before he died," Mr. Glennie continued, "Mr. Aldobrand lost all of his wealth except the money your diamond brought him. He left that money for you, hoping it would free him from the curse."

And so all of that great fortune became mine. But I never kept a penny for myself. Instead, we gave some to old sailors who needed it the most, and the rest was used to build a new lighthouse above Moonfleet Bay, to guide ships lost in storms.

I married Grace, and we spent our days walking in the woods, as we had years ago. I am older now, and happy. But I will never forget Elzivir. On stormy nights, I sit and watch the waves crash over Moonfleet Bay and remember the night that my friend saved me.

About *Moonfleet*

Moonfleet was written in
1898, by John Meade
Falkner, an English
novelist and poet. He
based the village of
Moonfleet on East Fleet,
a fishing village in
Dorset, on the south coast
of England. Carisbrook Castle,
where John finds Blackbeard's treasure,
is on the Isle of Wight. It really was used
as a prison in the 17th century, and has
a small room, with a deep, dark well...

Series editor: Lesley Sims

Designed by Natacha Goransky

First published in 2007 by Usborne Publishing Ltd., Usborne House,
83-85 Saffron Hill, London EC1N 8RT, England. www.usborne.com
Copyright © 2007 Usborne Publishing Ltd. The name Usborne and
the devices ♀ ⊕ are Trade Marks of Usborne Publishing Ltd.